the *Fear* factor Cookbook

PRICE STERN SLOAN

Designed by Shane Breaux

PRICE STERN SLOAN
Published by the Penguin Group
Penguin Group (USA) Inc., 375 Hudson Street, New York, New York 10014, U.S.A.
Penguin Group (Canada), 90 Eglinton Avenue East, Suite 700, Toronto, Ontario, Canada M4P 2Y3 (a division of Pearson Penguin Canada Inc.
Penguin Books Ltd, 80 Strand, London WC2R 0RL, England
Penguin Ireland, 25 St Stephen's Green, Dublin 2, Ireland
(a division of Penguin Books Ltd)
Penguin Group (Australia), 250 Camberwell Road, Camberwell, Victoria 3124, Australia
(a division of Pearson Australia Group Pty Ltd)
Penguin Books India Pvt Ltd, 11 Community Centre, Panchsheel Park, New Delhi - 110 017, India
Penguin Group (NZ), Cnr Airborne and Rosedale Roads, Albany, Auckland 1310, New Zealand
(a division of Pearson New Zealand Ltd)
Penguin Books (South Africa) (Pty) Ltd, 24 Sturdee Avenue, Rosebank, Johannesburg 2196, South Africa

Penguin Books Ltd, Registered Offices:
80 Strand, London WC2R 0RL, England

Fear Factor ™ & © 2006 Endemol Netherlands B.V. Used under license by Penguin Young Readers Group. All rights reserved. Published by
Price Stern Sloan, a division of Penguin Young Readers Group, 345 Hudson Street, New York, New York 10014. *PSS!* is a registered trademark o
Penguin Group (USA) Inc. Printed in Singapore.

Library of Congress Cataloging-in-Publication Data

Bennett, Bev.
The fear factor cookbook / recipes by Bev Bennett ; additional text by Siobhan Ciminera ;
illustrated by Adrian C. Sinnott ; photographs by David Mager/Pearson Learning Group.
p. cm.
Includes bibliographical references and index.
ISBN 0-8431-2013-4 (pbk. : alk. paper)
1. Cookery. I. Title.
TX652.B3958 2006
641.5—dc22
2005029414
10 9 8 7 6 5 4 3 2 1

the Fear factor Cookbook

Recipes by Bev Bennett
Additional text by Siobhan Ciminera
Illustrated by Adrian C. Sinnott
Photography by David Mager/Pearson Learning Group

PRICE STERN SLOAN

So you're a huge fan of *Fear Factor* and nothing can scare you, right? You watch the show every night on TV and all those sensational stunts and disgusting dares aren't enough to make you change the channel. But do you have the stomach for *The Fear Factor Cookbook*? Perhaps you'd like some Pig's Brain Pancakes for breakfast? What about a slice of Putrid Pizza for lunch, with a tall, refreshing glass of Ant Attack Ade? And don't forget to eat a healthy dinner of Eyeball Kabobs with a side of Sand Crab Snacks.

If you're still reading, then you're ready for the next frighteningly funny step—making these delectable dishes and more. Inside this book you'll find more than twenty-five outrageous, easy-to-create recipes. Each one is made to look gross but taste delicious. Fun for the whole family, these recipes can be used for everyday meals or for entertaining guests. So, if fear is not a factor for you, turn the page, grab a fork, and dig in—if you dare!

Table of Contents

Rancid Rules to Remember 6

The Get-Bugged Buffet 9

The Heart* of the Meal 37

Sea Spew 45

Serving Suggestions to Make You Shriek 60

Index 64

*As well as bile, brains, and other body parts!

Rancid Rules to Remember

Throughout the book, you'll see this symbol ![symbol] next to steps that should be done by an adult. The kitchen can be a very fun place, but it is also a place with hot appliances and sharp tools. Never work in the kitchen without an adult present, and always ask permission.

* Make sure you follow the directions for each recipe closely and measure ingredients carefully.

* Don't get stuck—gather all the ingredients and supplies together before beginning any recipe.

* The *Fear Factor* dishes in this book turn weird colors because the recipes often include food dyes, not because the food is rotten. To prevent food from spoiling and making you sick, keep perishable ingredients such as milk, meat, cheese, and eggs in the refrigerator, and always check the expiration date before using any ingredient.

* Protect your clothes and yourself—wear an apron whenever you're working in the kitchen and roll up long sleeves and pull back long hair before working over the stove.

* When using a saucepan, never leave the handle hanging over the edge of the stove. Always push the handle in so it hangs over the stove but not over a hot burner.

* When using a knife, never cut directly on the counter. Always use a clean cutting board.

* Don't reuse utensils until you wash them well with soap and water. You don't want to spread bacteria. This is especially important when working with raw meat.

* Always use pot holders when handling anything hot.

🦟 Wash all fruits and vegetables thoroughly.

🦟 Never leave the kitchen without making sure that the stove, oven, and all appliances are off.

🦟 Don't serve a *Fear Factor* recipe with hard ingredients, such as nuts or hard candies, to children under age two. They may accidentally choke on hard pieces of food.

🦟 Some people are very allergic to nuts. Before serving any recipe with nuts in it, make sure no one is allergic. If someone is, it's very easy to substitute another ingredient. See individual recipes for some suggestions.

🦟 You can make every dish in this book using only edible ingredients. Never add anything to a *Fear Factor* dish that you can't eat.

🦟 Serving *Fear Factor* meals and snacks to your friends is fun as you watch them turn green in disgust. But eating is serious business. Don't joke around when you have food in your mouth.

🦟 Don't let your kitchen get frightening—always clean up when you are finished and make sure to put all perishable items back in the refrigerator.

🦟 It's fun to play in the dirt, but don't bring it into the kitchen. Always wash your hands well with soap and water before beginning any recipe.

Most of the recipes in this book are vegetarian or have meat ingredients that are easily omitted. But for you vulgar vegetarians, the following few recipes are primarily meat-based: Tasty Tarantula Treats, Pig's Brain Pancakes, Bloody Rat Legs, Rat Stew, and the Giant Sea Slug Sandwich.

When you're stocking your *Fear Factor* kitchen, you may not find all the gruesome ingredients in the package sizes the recipes call for. Don't worry. Use an amount closest to what the recipe calls for. Adding a little more or less of some ingredient won't hurt the finished dish.

Crawling All Over the World

If you thought eating food that looks like bugs is gross, you'll freak out when you see what people actually eat all over the world!

Central Africa	India	Mexico
Locust Cakes	Red Ants with Rice	Caterpillars
Australia	**Japan**	**Java**
Roasted Grubs	Earthworm Pies	Fried Dragonflies
China	**Brazil**	**France**
Fried Grasshoppers	Tarantulas	*Escargot* (Snails)

Chapter 1

The Get-Bugged Buffet

Creepy-Crawly Cake

This muddy dish is the perfect down-in-the-dirt dessert.

INGREDIENTS:
1 prepared angel food cake (see note)
1 (1-pound) can chocolate-fudge frosting
1 ¹/₂ cups heavy cream
3 tablespoons unsweetened cocoa powder
6 tablespoons confectioners' sugar
12 gummy worms in green, red, and yellow colors

SUPPLIES:
Bread knife
Electric mixer
Spoon

1. Place cake on a work surface. Using a bread knife, cut off the top third of the cake and set aside. This is the lid.

2. Pull out the insides of the cake, leaving a wall about $1/2$ inch thick. Pull out some of the insides of the lid, too.

3. Frost the outside of both the lid and the cake with the chocolate-fudge frosting. Freeze the cake and lid for 1 hour or until the frosting is firm. This makes the cake easier to handle.

4. For the muddy cake filling, combine the cream, cocoa powder, and confectioners' sugar in the electric mixer bowl. Stir by hand with a spoon until cocoa is mixed in. Beat at high speed with the electric mixer for 1 minute or until the cream is stiff.

5. Spoon the whipped cream mud into the bottom of the cake and the lid.

6. Arrange half of the worms in the whipped cream so they hang out the sides. Top with the lid, setting it at a slight angle so you can see the worms. Arrange the remaining worms so they're crawling up the sides of the cake.

Serves 10 as dessert.

Not ready for dessert yet? You can make this cake up to 4 hours ahead of time and refrigerate it.

NOTE: Angel food cake comes in several sizes, from 7 to 9 inches across. The recipe has enough muddy cake filling and frosting to fill a larger 9-inch cake.

Ewww factor Serve this cake on a platter of dirt. Place 10 to 15 thin, crispy chocolate cookies in a plastic bag. Roll with a rolling pin to crush into cookie crumb dirt. Spread the dirt on a serving tray and add a few gummy worms. Place the cake on top of the dirt.

Crushed Grasshopper Guacamole

Great gourmets love a good snack. This one will leave everyone at your table chirping for more!

INGREDIENTS:
2 medium-size ripe avocados, divided
$1/8$ teaspoon garlic salt
1 teaspoon lime juice
2 tablespoons chopped onion
3 cups blue tortilla chips
1 cup shredded lettuce
2 or 3 small black olives without pits
1 small jicama (see note)

SUPPLIES:
Sharp knife
Spoon
Fork
Small bowl
Serving plate
Melon baller or teaspoon
Dinner knife

1. Cut one avocado in half with a sharp knife. Remove the pit. With a spoon, scoop out the insides into a small bowl.

2. Mash the avocado with a fork. Stir in the garlic salt, lime juice, and onion with a spoon. Set aside.

3. Spread the tortilla chips on a serving plate. Spread the lettuce over the chips. Gently spread the guacamole over the lettuce.

4. Cut the second avocado in half with a sharp knife and remove the pit. Use a melon baller or teaspoon to scoop out avocado balls. You should get about 12 balls, which will be the grasshopper heads.

5. With a dinner knife, make grasshopper mouths by making a small slash on the bottom of each head. Cut the olives into small bits and press them onto the grasshopper heads for the eyes.

6. Peel the jicama with a dinner knife and cut off very thin sticks for legs. Make little cuts in the legs for grasshopper feelers. Scatter the legs over the guacamole. Serve immediately.

Serves 4 as a snack.

NOTE: Jicama is a tan vegetable with crisp, white flesh. It's often used in Mexican dishes. You can find it in the produce section of your supermarket. If you can't find one, substitute a parsnip, which looks like a carrot with the blood sucked out until it's been bleached white.

Ewww factor Measure ¼ teaspoon hot red pepper sauce into an eyedropper or small spoon and sprinkle over the guacamole for grasshopper goo. Don't overdo it. This sauce is very hot.

13

Tasty Tarantula Feast

Want to get tangled up in a good meal? Try this for dinner.

INGREDIENTS:
1 ½ cups shredded sweetened coconut
1 pound raw turkey Italian sausage meat
1 (8.1-ounce) package pad thai meal kit
¼ cup roasted peanuts
Chow mein noodles

SUPPLIES:
Baking sheet
Large plate
Large pot
Wooden spoon
Spoon

1. Preheat oven to 350 degrees and spread the coconut on a baking sheet. Toast the coconut in the oven for 5 minutes or until lightly browned, shaking once or twice during cooking.

2. Remove from the oven. Pour the coconut onto a large plate.

3. Remove the sausage from the meat casings. Form 32 small meatballs.

4. To make the ugliest, hairiest tarantula bodies, roll a few meatballs at a time in the toasted coconut to cover.

5. Place the tarantula bodies on the baking sheet. Bake for 15 minutes or until the turkey is completely cooked, turning the meatballs over after 10 minutes.

6. Meanwhile, to make a pile of vile spiderwebs for the tarantulas, bring 3 quarts of water to a boil in a large pot.

7. Add the transparent noodles (the vile spiderwebs) from the kit to the water. Cook for 4 to 6 minutes, or until tender.

8. Drain the pot over the sink and into a colander. The pot will be very heavy, so you must get an adult to do this.

9. Return the noodles to the pot and add half the packet of pad thai sauce (the disgusting spider sauce) to the noodles and stir with a wooden spoon.

10. Add the roasted peanuts for spider droppings and stir again. Taste and add more of the pad thai sauce if you like. If anyone is allergic to nuts, skip the peanuts.

11. Spoon the spiderwebs onto 4 plates. Top each with 8 tarantula meatballs.

12. Stick 8 chow mein noodles into each tarantula body for the spider legs.

Serves 8 for dinner.

NOTE: If you can't find a pad thai meal kit, cook 8 ounces of transparent noodles and toss with 3 to 4 tablespoons of hoisin sauce. Both ingredients are available in the Asian section of the supermarket.

Ewww factor
Drizzle a little hot chile and garlic sauce (like Tabasco® sauce) over each serving for tarantula blood. Just use a little bit because this sauce is very hot.

Ant Attack Ade

**What's worse than ants in your pants?
Ants in your drink!**

INGREDIENTS:
1 cup sliced strawberries
1 (6-ounce) carton vanilla or strawberry yogurt
2 teaspoons honey
$\frac{1}{2}$ cup orange juice
2 ice cubes
1 black or red licorice twist (like Twizzlers®)
Peanut butter

SUPPLIES:
Blender
Fancy glass
Scissors

1. To make the smoothie, combine the strawberries, yogurt, honey, orange juice, and ice cubes in a blender container.

2. Blend at high speed until mixture is frothy. Pour into a tall glass.

3. To make the ants, use a pair of scissors to cut bite-size pieces of licorice. Make 6 to 8 ants.

4. Arrange small dots of peanut butter on the outside of the glass. Stick the licorice ants on the peanut butter for an ant invasion!

5. Drink quickly so the ants don't attack your drink!

Serves 1 as a beverage.

Ewww factor Before serving, squeeze some black or red decorating gel (depending on the color of your ants) onto the smoothie. It'll look like some of the ants were blended in.

Tomato Hornworm Juice

Add a crispy, crunchy critter to your drink!

INGREDIENTS:
3 tablespoons whipped cream cheese
2 drops green food coloring
1 (6- to 8-inch-long) curved green bean
1 small pointed piece of raw carrot
1 cup (8 ounces) tomato juice

SUPPLIES:
Small bowl
Fancy glass

1. Combine 2 tablespoons of cream cheese and green food coloring in a small bowl.

2. Using your hands, gently spread cream cheese over the green bean to make a hornworm.

3. Shape the remaining tablespoon of cream cheese by hand into thin strips and arrange across the worm.

4. Add the carrot piece to one end of the worm for the "horn."

5. Pour the tomato juice into a fancy glass. Arrange the worm so it's balanced on top of the glass.

Serves 1 as a beverage.

NOTE: You can make as many worms and cocktails as you like. You can also make the worms ahead of time and store them in the refrigerator to gross out your parents.

Ewww factor What's worse than a worm in your drink? Half a worm. Make a second worm, but float half in the drink so it looks like someone's taken a bite out of it.

Slimy Centipede Salad

There are over 100 reasons why this meal is nauseating. Eat them all!

INGREDIENTS:
2 (7-inch) cucumbers
4 cups shredded lettuce
1 (8-ounce) carton whipped cream cheese
   with chives, or plain cream cheese
Green and yellow food coloring
1 or 2 baby carrots
1 package (about 2 ounces) fresh chives
Pretzel sticks

SUPPLIES:
Vegetable peeler
Dinner knife
4 salad plates
Electric mixer
Scissors

1. Peel the cucumbers with a vegetable peeler, and then cut the cucumbers in half lengthwise with a dinner knife.

2. Arrange the lettuce on 4 large salad plates as grass for your bugs. Place 1 cucumber half, cut side down, on each bed of lettuce.

3. Place the cream cheese in the bowl of an electric mixer. Add a few drops of green and yellow food coloring.

4. Using the electric mixer, mix the food coloring and the cream cheese together to make a light green skin for the centipede.

5. Divide the colorful cream cheese into 4 equal parts. Spread one part over each centipede.

6. Using a dinner knife, cut the carrots into 8 thin, round slices. Stand up 2 slices on one end of each centipede for the eyes.

7. Cut the chives into 2-inch strips with a pair of scissors, and press crosswise on the centipede bodies for stripes.

8. Break the pretzel sticks in half so that they're each about 2 inches long. Arrange the halves around the bottom of the centipede for legs. You probably won't get 100 legs into each centipede, so use as many as you like.

Serves 4 as a light lunch or as a dinner salad.

Ewww *factor*

You can shock everyone with a giant millipede. Start with a big seedless cucumber that is 12 to 14 inches long. Peel it and cut in half lengthwise as directed. Decorate and add twice the pretzel legs.

Madagascar Hissing Cockroach Cakes

Everyday desserts getting you down? Then reach for a snack that's sure to make you scream with delight!

INGREDIENTS:

6 golden sponge cakes with creamy center, prepackaged
1 (1-pound) can milk-chocolate frosting
6 malted milk balls
2 tubes black decorating gel
1 tube red decorating gel
1 plain chocolate candy bar or
    pretzel sticks or both

SUPPLIES:

Dinner knife
Paring knife

1. Place sponge cakes one at a time on a plate. With a dinner knife, spread the sponge cake with 2 tablespoons chocolate frosting or enough to completely cover with a thin coating.

2. Press 1 malted milk ball into one end of each cake for the cockroaches' heads.

3. Make stripes across the cockroach with the black gel. Put cockroach eyes on the malted milk ball using the red gel.

4. Using a paring knife, cut very thin sticks off the candy bar. Put 2 smaller sticks on either side of the malted milk ball for the cockroach's antennae and 3 sticks on either side of the sponge cake for the cockroach's legs. You can substitute pretzel sticks for the chocolate if you prefer.

Makes 6 desserts or snacks.

NOTE: To make the antennae, add a dab of chocolate frosting to the end of the sticks so that they stay in one place on the malted milk ball.

LESS SUGARY VARIATION:

If you've got a hankering for hissing cockroaches but don't want all that sugar, try this less-sweet alternative using crescent rolls.

1. Preheat oven to 375 degrees.

2. Start with an 8-ounce tube of refrigerated crescent rolls. Unwrap the rolls and drizzle about 1 teaspoon strawberry or cherry jam on the wide end of each roll for blood; then roll up from the wide end to the narrow tip.

3. Place on an ungreased baking sheet and bake for 11 to 13 minutes.

4. Decorate with frosting, thin chocolate candy slices, and pretzel sticks as directed above.

Ewww factor These bugs are called hissing cockroaches for a reason! Have fun with this recipe (and your guests) by hissing while everyone at your table tries to eat this disgustingly delicious dish.

Firm Worm Dessert

These worms aren't going anywhere—except into your mouth!

INGREDIENTS:
1 (3-ounce) package lemon-flavored gelatin
1 cup boiling water
12 to 16 brightly colored gummy worms
Vegetable oil

SUPPLIES:
Heatproof bowl
Wooden spoon
4 scallop-edged bowls
Paring knife
4 small plates

1. For worms floating in a putrid pool, place the gelatin in a heatproof bowl. Stir in boiling water and stir constantly with a wooden spoon until the gelatin is dissolved. Stir in 1 cup cold water.

2. Pour the gelatin "pool water" into 4 (1 cup each) scallop-edged bowls lightly coated with vegetable oil. Let cool to room temperature.

3. Add 3 or 4 worms to each pool. Refrigerate for 2 hours or until the putrid pools are firm.

 4. To serve, run a small paring knife around the inside each of each bowl. Turn the bowls upside down onto small serving plates.

Serves 4 as dessert.

Drizzle a little caramel sauce for rotting worm innards around the outside of each putrid pool after you unmold the gelatin. You can also add a few chunky caramel pieces to make the worm innards look less finely pureed.

Squirmy Wormy Spaghetti

The dish that looks right back at you!

INGREDIENTS:
$1/2$ teaspoon salt
1 (8.8-ounce) package udon noodles (see note)
2 tablespoons butter or margarine
$1/4$ teaspoon pepper, optional
Chunky spaghetti sauce
8 baby mozzarella balls (see note)
8 small black olives
   without the pits

SUPPLIES:
Large pot
Wooden spoon
Colander
Large fork
Plate
Spoon
Dinner knife

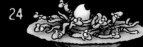

1. To make a bed of worms, fill a large pot with 2 quarts of water. Add the salt and bring to a boil over high heat.

2. Add the noodles and stir with a wooden spoon so they don't stick. Boil the noodles for 10 minutes or until tender.

3. To get rid of the water, drain the noodles into a colander. The pot will be very heavy, so you must get an adult to help.

4. Return the noodles to the pot. Add the butter and stir until it melts. Stir in the pepper.

5. Twirl the noodles around a large fork.

6. Place the worms on a plate, pushing the noodles off the fork with your fingers. Leave a hole in the center of the worms for the eye.

7. Spoon 1½ to 2 tablespoons spaghetti sauce into the center to resemble congealed blood. You can make a total of 8 worm beds on separate plates for a disgusting appetizer, or put 2 beds on each plate for a main course.

8. To make one decaying cow eye looking up at you from each bed of worms, make an indentation in each baby mozzarella ball with the tip of a dinner knife.

9. Add a black olive to each mozzarella ball to form the iris of the eyeball.

10. To make this dish just a little more disgusting, add more congealed blood sauce to each plate.

Serves 8 as an appetizer; 4 as a main course.

NOTE: Udon noodles are available in the Asian section of most supermarkets, or you can substitute 8 ounces of whole wheat spaghetti. Baby mozzarella balls are available in some supermarkets and most natural or fancy food stores.

Ewww **factor** Take a few black olives without pits and cut into small, thin ant-size pieces. Sprinkle these "ants" in the worm beds.

Delectable, Edible Bugs

In case there just aren't enough insect dishes to whet your whistle, here are a few more very simple bugs that you can eat as snacks, use to prank your friends, or use to decorate any dish.

NOTE: The bugs on these pages are really fun and easy to make. And the techniques discussed in these recipes can be used to make all sorts of different bugs. Have fun decorating them however you want, but always remember to never use any material that isn't edible in your bugs. And always make sure no one is allergic to nuts before serving any of these bugs.

Slugs

INGREDIENTS:
3 tablespoons smooth peanut butter
2 tablespoons confectioners' sugar
Green food coloring
Cake sprinkles in the color of your choice

SUPPLIES:
Bowl

1. Combine the peanut butter and sugar in a small bowl. Work the mixture with your hands to form a paste. This is peanut butter putty. (And to make your slugs green, add some food coloring to the mixture, too!)

2. Pinch off pieces the size of a garden slug, about $1/2$ to 1 inch long. Pinch the edges to come to points.

3. Add 2 sprinkles to one end of each slug for antennae.

Repeat for more slugs.

Worms

INGREDIENTS:
3 tablespoons smooth peanut butter
2 tablespoons confectioners' sugar
2 tubes black decorating gel
Cake sprinkles in the color of your choice

SUPPLIES:
Small bowl
Baking sheet
   or sheet of waxed paper

1. Combine the peanut butter and sugar in a small bowl. Work the mixture with your hands to form a paste. This is peanut butter putty.

2. Divide the peanut butter putty into 4 equal pieces and roll each into a rope about 5 inches long and $1/2$ inch wide.

3. Place on a lightly greased baking sheet or a sheet of waxed paper and form into a nasty squirming worm shape.

4. Make black stripes across the worm with the decorating gel. Use 2 cake sprinkles to make worm "horns" on one end of the body.

5. Place the baking sheet in the freezer for 1 hour or until the worms are firm.

NOTE: Peanut butter putty is the combination of peanut butter and confectioners' sugar used at the beginning of the slug and worm recipes. It's perfect for making slippery, slimy bugs. Go nuts making worms, slugs, caterpillars, and more! And that's not all—use this recipe for making snakes and eels, too. All you need is a little more peanut butter, a little more sugar, and the food coloring of your choice to make them as long, thick, and colorful as you like.

Scorpions

INGREDIENTS:
4 miniature marshmallows
Chow mein noodles
1 tube black decorating gel
Cake sprinkles in the color of your choice

SUPPLIES:
Wooden skewer

1. Take a wooden skewer and poke a hole through the center of 2 or 3 marshmallows, depending on how long you want your scorpion.

2. Gently push a long chow mein noodle through the marshmallows so they form a chain. If a noodle breaks, don't worry—just add another.

3. Hold either end of your scorpion and gently push up so that your scorpion has a slight "U" shape.

4. Poke a hole on either side of the head using a wooden skewer. Insert a small, curved piece of chow mein noodle into each hole to form the pincers.

5. Poke 3 holes on either side of the marshmallow "body" and insert 3 noodles of the same size to form the legs.

6. Gently coat the scorpion with decorating gel.

7. Add sprinkles to the head for eyes.

8. Refrigerate the scorpion for 1 hour to firm up the gel.

Makes 1 scorpion.

Don't stop at scorpions—marshmallow chains can be used to make all sorts of insects. For instance, make an ant by stringing 3 marshmallows together and coating them with black decorating gel. And the best part about marshmallow chains is that you can make your bugs as long as you like!

Cicadas

INGREDIENTS:
$\frac{1}{2}$ cup semisweet chocolate chips
1 teaspoon solid vegetable shortening
15 plain almonds
Green or red fruit leather
Red cake sprinkles (or any color you want!)

SUPPLIES:
Small pot
Wooden spoon
Baking sheet or waxed paper
Dinner knife

1. Combine the chocolate chips and shortening in a small, dry pot.

2. Heat the mixture over the lowest setting on the stove for 1 to 2 minutes, stirring constantly with a wooden spoon until the chocolate melts and is the consistency of mud. Your melted chocolate will stay this way for about 30 minutes until it begins to firm up, so work quickly.

3. Stir the almonds in the chocolate to coat.

4. Lightly grease a baking sheet or a sheet of waxed paper. Scoop the almonds out of the pot and place them onto the baking sheet. Set aside for 15 minutes, or until the chocolate just begins to firm up. The almond forms the cicada body.

5. With a dinner knife, cut 30 wings, each about 1 inch long and $\frac{1}{2}$ inch wide, from the fruit leather. Place 1 wing on either side of each body and gently press in.

6. Place 2 cake sprinkles on one end of the almond to form the cicada's eyes.

7. Set aside at room temperature for 1 hour, or until chocolate is completely set. You can also freeze the cicadas to firm up the chocolate.

Makes 15 cicadas.

NOTE: You'll probably have some leftover chocolate. You can drizzle it in thin strips onto the baking sheet. Once the chocolate cools, you'll have delicious legs for different bugs.

NOTE: Dipping nuts in melted chocolate and covering them with fruit leather is a technique that can be used to make all sorts of bugs with wings to really gross everyone out. Just use your imagination, and you can make cockroaches, beetles, and more!

World Traveler's Buffet

If you're planning a trip around the world, make sure to look out for these items on the menu. And always be careful whenever anyone says, "Tastes like chicken!"

Australia
Bat

France
Grilled Rat

China
Bear Paws

Germany
Blood Pudding

Scotland
Haggis*

Taiwan
Ape Brains

Texas
Armadillo

*What exactly is haggis? First, a sheep's heart, lungs, and liver are mixed with oatmeal and fat. Then the combination is placed in the sheep's stomach and boiled in a pot of water. Mmm, sounds tasty, right?

Chapter 2

The Heart* of the Meal

*As well as bile, brains, and other body parts

Pig's Brain Pancakes

Eat up! Brains are a great source of protein *and* a great way to start your day.

INGREDIENTS:

$2/3$ cup milk, or more if necessary
2 tablespoons melted butter
1 egg, beaten
Green food coloring
1 cup flour
2 teaspoons baking powder
$1/4$ teaspoon salt
1 tablespoon sugar
Butter for frying
4 slices ham, cut into thin strips
Raspberry sauce (see note)
Maple syrup, optional

SUPPLIES:

Small bowl
Spoon
Large bowl
Large skillet
Spatula
2 plates

1. For moldy pancakes, combine $^2/_3$ cup milk, melted butter, and egg in a small bowl. Add a few drops of food coloring and stir well.

2. Combine the flour, baking powder, salt, and sugar in a large bowl and stir well with a spoon. Add the milk mixture and stir to form a batter. If the batter is too thick to drop from a spoon, add a little more milk.

3. Melt 1 tablespoon of butter in a large, nonstick skillet.

4. Drop the moldy pancake batter by a $^1/_4$-cup measuring cup into the melted butter. Make 3 pancakes.

5. Cook the pancakes for 2 minutes, or until puffed, firm, and lightly browned. Flip the pancakes over with a spatula and cook the other side for 2 minutes.

6. Add 1 more tablespoon of butter, and cook the remaining batter to make 3 more pancakes. Arrange the pancakes on 2 plates.

7. For the pig's brain, form the ham into 2 piles, weaving the strips into a tangled mess of brain. Top each pancake stack with one pile of brain.

8. Squeeze a little raspberry sauce over the brain for pig's blood. Add maple syrup if you like.

Serves 2 for breakfast.

NOTE: Raspberry sauce is available in a squeeze bottle in the jam or ice-cream section of the supermarket. You can substitute green mint jelly for pig's bile, if you prefer. Just use a little, though, because the taste of mint can be very strong.

NOTE: If you don't have time to make the pancakes from scratch, add a few drops of green food coloring to instant pancake mix and start from step 3.

Ewww *factor*

Top the pancakes with eyeballs. To make the eyeballs, soften 2 tablespoons of butter. Stir in a little red food coloring for a red tint. Shape the butter into 4 small balls. Freeze for 30 minutes or until firm. Squeeze a tiny bit of black decorating sauce onto each eyeball for the pupil and add red decorating gel lines to make bloodshot eyes. Top each serving with 2 eyeballs.

Cow Tongue Chow

Everyone at the table will lick this tasty treat right up!

INGREDIENTS:
1 (1-pound) roll frozen loaf of white bread dough
1 egg white (see note)
Red food coloring
Red-colored sugar (see note)
Cherry or strawberry jam, optional
$1/2$ cup whipped cream cheese
Green food coloring

SUPPLIES:
Baking sheet
Fork
Small bowl
Basting brush
Spatula
Bread knife

Mooo!

1. Thaw the bread dough on a plate in the refrigerator for 6 hours, or until soft and pliable.

2. Place the loaf on a greased baking sheet. To form the revolting cow tongue, pull the dough into a strip about 10 inches long. Make a deep indentation down the center for the "groove" in the tongue. The "tip" of the tongue should be about 1 inch wide; the opposite end of the tongue should be about 3 inches wide. Set aside for 1 hour for the tongue to get big and puffy. As the dough rises, the tongue shape may disappear. If that happens, press down on the center groove of the tongue again.

3. Preheat the oven to 350 degrees.

4. Beat the egg white with a fork in a small bowl and add a few drops of red food coloring.

5. With a basting brush, gently brush the egg white on the tongue to turn it red. Sprinkle generously with red sugar. If you'd like a bloody tongue, spoon a little cherry jam for the blood in the groove of the tongue.

6. Bake for 25 minutes, or until the tongue is firm and high.

7. Remove the tongue from the oven. Use a spatula to loosen it from the baking sheet. Cool on the baking sheet for 5 minutes. Then remove the tongue to a wire rack to completely cool.

8. While the tongue is cooling, make a bile spread. Combine the cream cheese and a few drops of green food coloring in a small bowl.

9. Slice the bread with a bread knife and serve with bile spread.

Serves 10 as part of a breakfast.

NOTE: Red-colored sugar is available in the baking section of the supermarket.

NOTE: To get the egg white for this dish, crack a raw egg against the side of a cup or bowl. The clear, gooey liquid that comes out first is the egg white. Gently pour it into the bowl, being careful so the yellow egg yolk doesn't slide into the bowl as well. You can throw the yolk away or refrigerate it for a couple of days to use in another dish.

Ewww factor

For a rotting and decaying cow tongue, drizzle on a little black decorating gel just before serving.

35

Blood and Bile Cocktail

What a terrifying and terrific treat—with eyeballs, bile, and blood, who could ask for more?

INGREDIENTS:

14 large seedless purple grapes, or enough to fill an ice-cube tray with 1 grape for each section

14 white chocolate chips, or enough for each grape

1 cup lemon-flavored drink

1 (3-ounce) package cherry-flavored gelatin

1 quart lime-flavored drink, chilled

SUPPLIES:

Sharp knife
Ice-cube tray
Heatproof bowl
Spoon
6 fancy glasses
Tray
Long-handled spoon

1. For cow eyeballs, make a small hole in the stem end of each grape using the tip of a sharp knife.

2. For the pupil of the eye, press a white chocolate chip, pointy side first, into each grape.

3. Place each grape, chip side up, into a section of the ice-cube tray and pour in the lemon-flavored drink.

4. Place the ice-cube tray in the freezer and freeze at least 2 hours or until solid. You can do this the night before if you prefer.

5. For bloody goblets, place the gelatin in a heatproof bowl.

6. Pour in 1 cup of boiling hot water, and stir the gelatin with a spoon until all the powder mixes into the water.

7. Chill the gelatin in the refrigerator until it's as thick as oatmeal (about 45 minutes). Don't keep it in the refrigerator for too long, or your gelatin will be too firm to look like blood.

8. Take 6 fancy glasses, one at a time, and dip into the gelatin to coat the rims. The excess gelatin will drip down the sides of the glass like blood.

9. Place the glasses right-side up on a tray. Refrigerate for 1 hour, or overnight if you prefer.

10. To make the cocktails, pour bile (the lime-flavored drink) equally into the 6 glasses and add your cow-eye ice cubes to each glass.

Serve immediately.

Serves 6 as a beverage.

NOTE: Serve this drink with a long-handled spoon. For safety's sake, if the ice cubes melt before you are finished, scoop out the grapes and chocolate bits.

Ewww *factor*

As a special gross treat, add a gummy worm to each glass.

Cow's Blood Hot Chocolate

A comforting drink for every mooood!

INGREDIENTS:
$^1/_4$ cup sugar
2 tablespoons unsweetened cocoa powder
$^1/_2$ teaspoon red food coloring
2 cups milk, divided
4 marshmallows
2 maraschino cherries, cut in half
2 to 4 gummy worms

SUPPLIES:
Small saucepan
Spoon
2 heatproof glass mugs
Dinner knife
Long-handled spoon

1. To make cow's blood hot chocolate, combine the sugar, cocoa powder, red food coloring, and $^1/_4$ cup milk in a small saucepan. Stir with a spoon to mix well, and then add the remaining milk.

2. Cook over low heat, stirring occasionally until the milk is hot and the sugar is dissolved, about 2 to 5 minutes. Pour the milk into 2 heatproof glass mugs.

3. To top the drink with cow eyes, make a slight cut in each marshmallow. Press a cherry half into each to form the iris of the eye. Float on the drink.

4. For an extra-gross treat, wrap 1 or 2 gummy worms around the edge of the drink.

Serves 2 as a beverage.

NOTE: Serve this drink with a long-handled spoon. For safety's sake, do not drink until you've scooped out the marshmallows and cherries.

Ewww factor Use a tube of black decorating gel to decorate the glass with cockroach bile. Arrange 2 maraschino cherries for rat kidneys, and a worm on a wooden skewer and balance on the drink.

Eyeball Kabobs

Soft and chewy, tasty and gooey!

INGREDIENTS:
2 baby mozzarella balls (see note)
2 pistachio nuts or 2 small pieces dill pickle
1 black olive without the pit, cut into very thin strips
2 large cherry tomatoes
Tomato sauce or cocktail sauce
1 tablespoon mayonnaise or light mayonnaise
$1^1/_2$ teaspoons pesto (see note)

SUPPLIES:
Sharp knife
Wooden skewer
Toothpick
Small bowl

1. For cow eyes, make a hole in each mozzarella ball. Press a pistachio into them. For tree-frog eyes, make a hole in each tomato. Press the olive strips into them.

2. Push the cow eyes and frog eyes onto a wooden skewer, alternating them.

3. Dip a toothpick into tomato sauce and "paint" thin lines on the cheese to make the eyes look bloodshot.

4. Combine the mayonnaise and pesto to make bull's bile dipping sauce.

To serve, remove the eyeballs from the skewer and dip into the sauce. Do not eat the eyes straight from the skewer.

Serves 1 as a light lunch or dinner.

NOTE: Mozzarella balls are available in some supermarkets and natural or fancy food stores. Pesto is a combination of basil, olive oil, and pine nuts. You can also make bile by combining 1 tablespoon mayonnaise, 1 teaspoon mustard, and a few drops of green food coloring.

NOTE: Before serving, make sure no one is allergic to nuts. If so, use dill pickle pieces instead of pistachio bits and skip the pesto.

Ewww factor Infected eyeballs are even more disgusting. Break a few chow mein noodles into pieces and press them into the frog eyes.

Rat Stew

Looking for something to chew on?
Try this crunchy, scrumptious stew
made from only the best parts of the rat!

INGREDIENTS:
1 packed cup sauerkraut (see note)
1 pound ground beef
$\frac{1}{4}$ teaspoon salt
$\frac{1}{4}$ teaspoon pepper
1 tablespoon olive oil or vegetable oil
1 (25-ounce) jar of favorite pasta sauce
$\frac{1}{2}$ cup fried onion rings
8 black olives without pits, optional
4 cherry tomatoes cut in half, optional
Mozzarella cheese and/or radishes, optional

SUPPLIES:
Colander
Large plate
Bowl
Large skillet
Spoon
Deep platter

1. To make stringy, gross rat hair, place the sauerkraut in a colander and rinse under cold water. Squeeze out the water with your hands. Place the sauerkraut on a large plate and set aside.

2. Combine ground beef, salt, and pepper in a bowl. Shape the beef into balls the size of large jawbreaker candy. Roll the meatballs in the sauerkraut to form hairy rat meatballs.

3. Heat the oil in a very large nonstick skillet over medium heat.

4. Add the meatballs and cook, stirring with a spoon occasionally until the meat turns from red to brown on all sides (about 5 to 10 minutes).

5. Stir in any leftover sauerkraut and the pasta sauce. Reduce the heat to low and simmer the mixture for 10 minutes, stirring occasionally.

6. To serve, spoon the meatballs and sauce into a deep platter and sprinkle on onion rings for rat bones.

7. For rats' rotting heads, stuff each olive with half a tomato to resemble blood. Make a rat face by poking three holes in the olive (two for the eyes and a larger one for the mouth). Stuff tiny pieces of mozzarella cheese in the eye holes, and slivers of tomato in the mouth hole for lips.

Serves 4 for dinner.

NOTE: They call it sauerkraut for a reason—this is very smelly, very sour stuff. If you're brave enough, you can skip the rinsing step for a very stinky surprise. If you do so, you must make sure to still drain the sauerkraut of excess liquid.

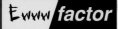 **Ewww factor** If you have beets in the refrigerator, slice off the long stem ends and use them to decorate your table. The "hairy" stem looks like a rat's tail and the inside of the beet is BLOOD red. Make sure no one eats them, though, as they are uncooked and tough.

Bloody Rat Legs

Picked fresh from the sewers, rat legs make a delicious dinner!

INGREDIENTS:
12 chicken wings
1 cup barbecue sauce, preferably a ketchup-based red sauce
2 cups chicken broth
1 cup uncooked rice
1 cooked chicken breast, skin removed
$\frac{1}{8}$ teaspoon each salt and pepper
2 tablespoons currants or raisins cut into small pieces

SUPPLIES:
Sharp knife
Baking sheet lined with aluminum foil
Basting brush
Small pot
Wooden spoon

1. Preheat the oven to 375 degrees. Cut each chicken wing in half at the joint using a sharp knife. The thick piece that looks like a chicken drumstick becomes a rat leg. Save the thin half of the wing for another recipe.

2. Place the rat legs on a baking sheet lined with aluminum foil.

3. With a basting brush, brush the legs with bloody barbecue sauce.

4. Bake for 35 minutes, or until completely cooked. Remove from the oven.

5. Meanwhile, to make a rice nest for the legs, bring the chicken broth to a boil over high heat in a small pot. Add the rice, and stir with a wooden spoon.

6. Reduce the heat to low, cover, and cook for 20 minutes, or until the rice is tender and the broth is absorbed.

7. Tear the chicken breast into bite-size pieces to look like the rat's body, and coat the pieces with the barbeque sauce.

8. Stir the chicken, salt, and pepper into the rice rat nest on the stove.

9. Spoon the rice onto a serving platter.

10. Sprinkle currants over the rice for rat droppings.

11. Arrange the bloody rat legs over the rice.

Serves 4 for dinner.

Ewww factor Decorate your dish with melted and bloody rat heads. Coat small mozzarella cheese balls with barbecue sauce. Place them under the broiler for about 1 minute. Make sure you don't leave them in too long or the cheese will lose its shape.

Deep-Sea Dining

Ever wonder what was once deep in the sea and is now on your plate? That's right, people all over the world enjoy these slimy, spiny snacks!

France
Boiled
Lamprey

Chile
Sea Urchins

Japan
Blowfish

China
Dried
Jellyfish

England
Jellied Eels

China
Smoked Sea
Cucumber

Chapter 3

Sea Spew

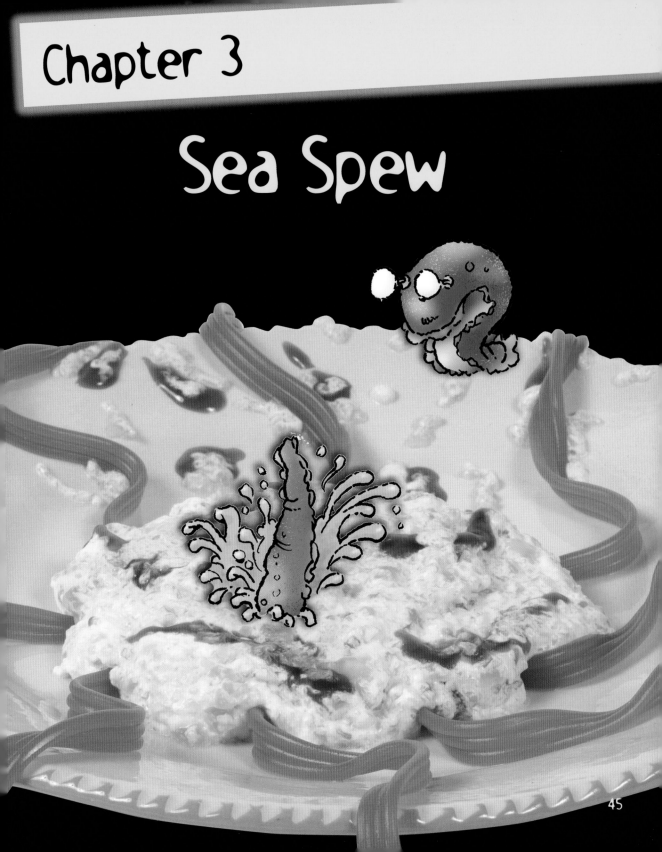

100-Year-Old Eggs

Start your day off right by scrambling up some octopus eggs aged to perfection.

INGREDIENTS:
1 small block mozzarella cheese at room temperature
1 tablespoon butter
1 cup coarsely chopped fresh spinach leaves
2 eggs
Blue and/or green food coloring
$\frac{1}{8}$ teaspoon salt
$\frac{1}{8}$ teaspoon pepper

SUPPLIES:
Vegetable peeler
Skillet
Spoon
Fork
Spatula

1. Using a vegetable peeler, peel off very thin, small slices of cheese.

2. Rub the cheese slices firmly between your hands until they are each about 1 inch long to form maggots. Make 8 to 10 maggots. Place the maggots on a dish and freeze while you're making the eggs.

3. Melt the butter in a nonstick skillet over medium heat. To infest the eggs with sea scum, add the spinach and cook for 1 to 2 minutes, stirring frequently with a spoon, or until limp.

4. Beat the eggs in a small bowl with a fork. Add 1 or 2 drops of blue food coloring (you know that yellow eggs and blue food coloring make green 100-year-old eggs, don't you?), or 1 drop of blue and 1 of green. Add the salt and pepper.

5. Pour the eggs into the skillet and cook over medium heat, stirring frequently with a spatula, until the eggs are firm and scrambled.

To serve, spoon the eggs onto a plate and sprinkle with maggots.

Serves 1 for breakfast.

Put ketchup in a squeeze bottle with a narrow opening and gently trickle it onto the eggs to resemble blood.

Scrumptious Squid Slush

Straight from the sea and onto your plate!

INGREDIENTS:
4 tomatoes
4 lettuce leaves
2 celery stalks
1 cup cooked baby shrimp, optional
4 black olives without pits
Cream cheese
Chow mein noodles

SUPPLIES:
4 salad plates
Dinner knife

1. To make a bed of bloody fish guts for the squid, cut the tomatoes into uneven, chunky pieces with a dinner knife.

2. Line 4 salad plates with lettuce to form a seaweed base.

3. Divide the tomato fish guts evenly into 4 portions and place each one on a salad plate.

4. Cut off the ends of the celery with a dinner knife. Cut the celery stalks into very thin slices and sprinkle around the fish guts to form sea worms.

5. You can also sprinkle the baby shrimp around the fish guts. Since shrimp are sold headless, this will look as if the octopus already bit the heads off each shrimp.

6. To make the squid, stand one olive in the center of each bed of fish guts for the head.

7. Using the tip of a dinner knife, add dots of cream cheese for the eyes.

8. Tuck 8 medium-size chow mein noodles under each olive with part of the noodles sticking out for the arms. Tuck 2 longer chow mein noodles in the back of the squid for the feeding tentacles.

Serves 4 as a salad.

To make squid "vomit," add little bits of mild tomato salsa to the bloody fish guts.

Slippery Octopus Salad

Eating this salad is not for the faint of heart!

INGREDIENTS:
1 cup chopped fresh spinach
1 small tomato
1/4 cup whipped cream cheese or
    chive-flavored cream cheese
Green food coloring
Blue food coloring
2 pimiento-stuffed green olives
Cooked green fettuccine

SUPPLIES:
Plate
Dinner knife
Bowl
Spoon

1. To make a seaweed bed for the octopus, place the spinach in the center of a serving plate.

2. Cut the top of the tomato off with a dinner knife to make a level surface and place the tomato upside down on the spinach bed.

3. In a bowl, mix 1 drop of both blue and green food coloring with the cream cheese until the mixture is a smooth sea-green color.

4. Spread the colored cream cheese on the tomato with a dinner knife to completely cover it. This is the octopus's head.

5. Press an olive into each side of the front of the octopus to create the eyes.

6. Form 8 legs by tucking the fettuccine under the octopus's head.

To serve, cut the octopus's head into pieces and toss with the seaweed, tentacles, and legs. Drizzle the dressing of your choice over the salad.

Serves 2 as a salad.

NOTE: If you like, flavor the plain cream cheese by adding some finely chopped, cooked bacon. Your octopus will look a little lumpy, as if it had some vile sea disease.

NOTE: When making the octopus's legs, decide how much fettuccine you'd like to use. For a decoration, use a single strand per leg. For a filling dish, twist several strands together. You can also use twice as much spinach for a substantial salad that will make your mom proud that you're eating your vegetables, no matter how gross!

Ewww *factor*

Weave a few cooked baby shrimp into the fettuccine to look like the unfortunate victims of the octopus.

Sea Slug Smoothie

A surprise in every sip!

INGREDIENTS:
1 medium-size ripe banana
1 (6-ounce) carton vanilla yogurt
$\frac{1}{4}$ cup milk
2 ice cubes
Red, green, yellow, and blue food coloring
1 blue, green, or yellow prepared gelatin dessert
   cup, or leftover fruit-flavored gelatin

SUPPLIES:
Blender
Tall glass
Dinner knife
Long-handled spoon

 1. To make the smoothie, combine the banana, yogurt, milk, and ice cubes in a blender container. Blend at high speed until the mixture is frothy.

 2. Add a drop of red, green, yellow, and blue food coloring and blend again for 30 seconds to make a loathsome-looking, mud-colored drink. Pour into a tall glass.

3. For the sea slug topping, cut the gelatin with a dinner knife into 6 small slivers and float on the smoothie.

Serves 1 as a beverage.

NOTE: Serve this drink with a long-handled spoon. For safety's sake, do not drink until you've scooped out the gelatin slivers.

Ewww factor Using a can of whipped cream, spray a thin line of cream around the rim of the glass. Cover the whipped topping with black or red decorating gel to make a slimy sea worm crawling up the glass.

Sand Crab Snacks

Eat these critters before they eat you!

INGREDIENTS:
4 curved potato or soy chips (like Pringles®)
$1/3$ cup cheddar cheese spread
16 whole salted cashews
4 small pimiento-stuffed olives

1. To make the crabs, turn the chips so the underside (the concave side) faces you. Spread 1 tablespoon of the cheese spread around the edges of the chip.

2. Split all the cashews in half along the seams. Arrange 2 cashew halves, 1 on each side, at one end of the cheese spread to form pincers. Arrange 6 cashew halves, 3 on each side, to form crab legs. Press in the legs and pincers. If anyone is allergic to nuts, use pretzel sticks instead of cashews.

3. Turn the crabs right-side up so they stand on their legs. Add 2 small dabs of the remaining cheese spread to the pincer end of the chip.

4. Slice each olive to make 2 thin pieces. Stand 1 olive slice on each cheese dab for crab eyes. Repeat for other crabs.

Serves 4 as a snack.

NOTE: Make sure to put these critters right out. The cheese makes the chips get soggy.

Ewww factor For jellyfish, make 1 package of lemon-flavored gelatin. After the gelatin has set, scoop out blobs, and place around plate. For tentacles, squeeze strands of honey mixed with raspberry dessert sauce coming out of the blobs.

Putrid Pizza

A smelly, stinky pizza straight from the sea!

INGREDIENTS:

1 (13.8-ounce) tube refrigerated pizza dough
1 (15.5-ounce) jar pizza sauce
4 mozzarella cheese sticks or 1 mozzarella cheese ball
1 (2-ounce) jar anchovy fillets, rinsed and drained
16 small mushrooms
$1/4$ cup whipped cream cheese
2 tablespoons blue cheese crumbles
1 to 2 teaspoons milk
Green or blue food coloring, optional
10 cherry tomatoes
1 package (about 2 ounces) fresh chives

SUPPLIES:

Baking sheet
Dinner knife
Paring knife
Bowl
Fork
Spoon
Scissors

1. Preheat the oven to 400 degrees. Unwrap the pizza dough and spread on a baking sheet to form a 10 by 13 inch crust. Bake for 5 minutes. Remove from the oven.

2. For the rotten, putrid topping, spread the pizza sauce over the crust.

3. Make fish skeletons from cheese by cutting 8 ($1/4$-inch-thick) slices of cheese from one cheese stick with a dinner knife. These are the skulls. Then cut thin cheese strips for the fish bones. You can make fish skeletons from the mozzarella ball by cutting thin cheese sticks or circles for skulls. Place the skulls on the pizza sauce, then form skeleton bodies from the cheese strips.

4. Arrange the putrid anchovy fillets over the pizza.

5. Cut the tops off the mushrooms with a dinner knife. Scatter these turtle shells around the pizza.

6. Bake for 10 minutes, or until the cheese melts and the sauce is hot. Remove from the oven.

7. While the pizza is baking, prepare sea urchins to top the pizza. Combine the cream cheese and blue cheese crumbles in a bowl and mash with a fork to form the sea urchin guts. Add a little milk to make the guts creamy. You can turn the guts green or blue with a couple of drops of food coloring if you like.

8. Cut the top third off of each tomato with a dinner knife to form the urchin bodies. Using your fingers, pull out the seeds and fibers. Spoon about 1 teaspoon of the cream cheese guts into each tomato.

9. Cut roughly ten 1-inch pieces from the chives. Stick in the cheese-filled tomato for tentacles standing in the guts. Repeat for each tomato.

10. Fill all the tomatoes and place on top of the pizza. You can also serve the sea urchins on the side or before the pizza as an "unappetizer."

Serves 6 as a dinner entrée or 12 as a party snack.

 **Ewww** *factor* Use a mild green salsa and drop by the $1/2$ teaspoonful on the baked pizza for rotting seaweed. Don't use more than a total of 3 teaspoons of salsa.

Giant Sea Slug Sandwich

It's just like eating a sausage, except *waaaay* more dangerous!

INGREDIENTS:

1 (10.1-ounce) tube refrigerated large
   crescent roll dough (6 to the tube)
6 (2- to 3-ounce) cooked sausages, such as
   Polish sausage or bratwurst (see note)
1 egg white (see note)
Green food coloring
2 large roasted red peppers, cut into thin strips
6 small pimiento-stuffed green olives
2 tablespoons mustard
1 tablespoon honey

SUPPLIES:

Fork
Basting brush
Dinner knife
Bowl
Spoon

1. Preheat the oven to 350 degrees. To make the sea slug bodies, unwrap the crescent roll dough and separate into individual pieces.

2. Place 1 sausage at the wide end of each roll. Roll up to the narrow tip.

3. You'll have some bare spots where the crust doesn't cover the sea slug. Press the dough with your fingers, pushing it over the bare patches. Place on a greased baking sheet. Repeat with the remaining dough and sausages.

4. In a bowl, beat the egg white with a fork and add a few drops of food coloring.

5. With a basting brush, gently brush the colored egg white on each slug to turn it a revolting green color.

6. Arrange pepper strips over each slug's body.

7. Cut each olive in half with a dinner knife and press 2 halves into one end of each slug for eyes.

8. Bake for 16 minutes, or until the slugs turn golden brown and green. Remove from the oven and set aside for 5 minutes.

9. Meanwhile, make poisonous slug dipping sauce for an accompaniment. Stir together mustard and honey in a bowl with a spoon. Add a drop or two of green food coloring.

Serves 6 as lunch or dinner.

NOTE: A curved sausage looks more like a slug. However, you can use frankfurters if you prefer.

NOTE: To get the egg white for this dish, crack a raw egg against the side of a cup or bowl. The clear, gooey liquid that comes out first is the egg white. Gently pour it into the bowl, being careful so the yellow egg yolk doesn't slide into the bowl as well. You can throw the yolk away or refrigerate it for a couple of days to use in another dish.

Ewww *factor* You can vary the skin color of the slugs to make a disgusting assortment. Divide the egg white into 3 bowls. Add a different food coloring to each bowl, and paint the slugs as directed.

The Great Big Blob

Be careful—the blob has been known to eat those who try to eat it!

INGREDIENTS:
1 (3-ounce) package lime gelatin
1 cup boiling water
$1/2$ cup heavy cream
2 tablespoons sugar
32 (6-inch) pieces red string licorice
Raspberry sauce

SUPPLIES:
Heatproof bowl
Spoon
Small bowl

1. To make the slimy sea blob's body, place the gelatin in a heatproof bowl. Stir in the boiling water with a spoon and stir constantly until the gelatin is dissolved.

2. Stir in 1 cup of cold water. Refrigerate for 2 hours, or until firm.

3. Beat the cream and sugar together with an electric mixer at medium-high speed to make whipped cream.

4. Stir the gelatin until it's in small lumps, and spoon the gelatin into the whipped cream.

5. Stir well until you get a speckled, light-green blob. Return to the refrigerator for 1 hour to firm up.

6. To form the whole blob, spoon the blob body onto 4 plates. Arrange 8 pieces of licorice for strangling tentacles at the base of the blob's body.

7. Drizzle a little raspberry sauce over each blob to look like its blood—or the blood of its prey.

Serves 4 as dessert.

Place a slug from page 26 in the blob's tentacles so it looks like a sea slug is being trapped by the blob.

Now that you can make bugs, slugs, blood, and mud, you're ready to have some real fun making full, foul feasts! We offer complete menus for breakfast, brunch, lunch, and dinner. Plus, don't miss our decorating suggestions to help make each meal a truly horrifying *Fear Factor* experience!

BREAKFAST for the Bold
Is everyone still asleep? This'll wake them up!

BEVERAGES:	ENTRÉES:	SIDE DISH:
Sea Slug Smoothie	Pig's Brain Pancakes	Cow Tongue Chow
Ant Attack Ade	100-Year-Old Eggs	

Decorating Ideas

CONSTRUCTION PAPER ANTS

1. Cut 3 big circles out of black construction paper.

2. Cut out 6 legs from black construction paper.

3. Tape the circles together and add the 6 legs.

4. Using chalk or white crayon, add a face to your ant.

MAGGOTS CRAWLING ON THE TABLE

1. Follow the directions for making maggots from the 100-Year-Old Eggs recipe using leftover mozzarella.

2. Place the maggots all over the table so that the table is covered with creepy critters.

SLUG-HEAD STREAMERS

1. Cut out a triangle from construction paper (any color). This is the slug head.

2. Decorate your slug head with eyes and a mouth.

3. Tape it to the end of a long streamer.

4. Hang the streamer from the ceiling.

PEANUT BUTTER PUTTY PIG BRAINS

1. Follow the directions on page 26 for making peanut butter putty.

2. Add a little red food coloring so that the putty turns pink, and roll approximately 8 pieces, each about 5 inches long.

3. Intertwine the pieces to look like a pile of brains.

Crunch and Munch BRUNCH

With all the creepy-crawly items on this menu,
you'll have trouble trying to grab a bite!

BEVERAGES:
Cow's Blood Hot Chocolate
Tomato Hornworm Juice

SIDE DISH:
Crushed Grasshopper
Guacamole

ENTRÉES:
Scrumptious Squid Slush
Slimy Centipede Salad

DESSERT:
Creepy-Crawly Cake

Decorating Ideas

Want to make this meal even more memorable? You can start by littering the table with extra tomato hornworms. And don't stop there—this meal is all about legs and tentacles, so go crazy. Print out or draw pictures of centipedes, millipedes, grasshoppers, squids, and octopuses, and put them up around the dining room. There's nothing better than having a gallery of leggy guests watch you and your friends eat!

Make 'Em Scream LUNCH

Lunch is the perfect time to play with your food!

BEVERAGE:
Blood and Bile Cocktail

ENTRÉES:
Eyeball Kabobs
Giant Sea Slug Sandwich
Putrid Pizza

SIDE DISH:
Sand Crab Snacks

DESSERT:
The Great Big Blob

Decorating Ideas

Want to have even more fun with this meal? It's as simple as adding eyeballs to the chairs and a giant sea slug to the table. With a lunch this gross, everyone will be begging for seconds!

EYEBALL DECORATIONS

1. Cut a circle out of white construction paper.

2. Draw a black pupil in the middle of the circle.

3. To make the eye bloodshot, draw squiggly red lines from the pupil to the edge of the circle.

4. Put 1 eyeball on the back of each chair.

GIANT SEA SLUG DECORATION

1. Gather enough pieces of green construction paper so that they stretch from one end of the table to the other.

2. Tape the pieces together.

3. Cut both ends of the paper chain so they form a point.

4. Pick one end to be the head and one end to be the tail. Draw eyes on the head.

5. Decorate the sea slug's body any way you like with stripes and blotches.

6. Place the giant sea slug on the table.

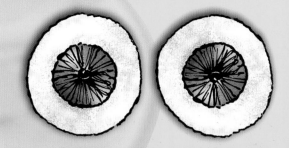

Dine if You Dare DINNER

What could be better than sitting down to this dinner at the end of a long, hard day?

APPETIZER:

Slippery Octopus Salad

ENTRÉES:

Tasty Tarantula Feast
Squirmy Wormy Spaghetti
Bloody Rat Legs
Rat Stew

DESSERTS:

Firm Worm Dessert
Madagascar Hissing Cockroach Cakes

Decorating Ideas

And there's more you can do to gross everyone out, like making web place mats and decorating the room with rat tails. It'll certainly be a feat if everyone can go to sleep after this meal!

WEB PLACE MATS

1. Cut out 12 strips about 10 inches long from white construction paper.

2. Intertwine them until they form a small spiderweb, and glue the pieces together.

3. Make enough for everyone at your table and put one at each place setting.

RAT TAILS

1. Cut out thin strips about 5 inches long from pieces of brown, gray, black, and white construction paper.

2. Cut one end of each strip so that it forms a point.

3. To make the rat tails hairy, add little scraps of the same color cloth in random places. It'll look like your rat tail has been chewed a little! EWWW!

4. Decorate the walls, tables, and chairs with your rat tails.

Index

100-Year-Old Eggs, 46

A
Almonds
  Cicadas, 29
Anchovies
  on Putrid Pizza, 54
Angel food cake
  Creepy-Crawly Cake, 10
Ant Attack Ade, 16
Avocados
  in Guacamole, 12

B
Bananas
  in Sea Slug Smoothie, 52
Barbecue sauce
  on Bloody Rat Legs, 42
Beans
  see Tomato Hornworm Juice, 17
Blood and Bile Cocktail, 36
Bloody Rat Legs, 42
Bratwurst
  see Giant Sea Slug Sandwich, 56
Bread
  Cow Tongue Chow, 34

C
Cakes
  Creepy-Crawly Cake, 10
  Madagascar Hissing Cockroach Cakes, 20
Carrots
  in Slimy Centipede Salad, 18
  in Tomato Hornworm Juice, 17
Cashews
  in Sand Crab Snacks, 53
Celery
  in Scrumptious Squid Slush, 48
Cheese
  on 100-Year-Old Eggs, 46
  in Eyeball Kabobs, 39
  on Putrid Pizza, 54
  in Rat Stew, 40
  in Sand Crab Snacks, 53
  in Squirmy Wormy Spaghetti, 24
Cherries
  in Cow's Blood Hot Chocolate, 38
Chicken
  Bloody Rat Legs, 42
Chives
  in Putrid Pizza, 54
  in Slimy Centipede Salad, 18
Chocolate
  on Cicadas, 29
  Cow's Blood Hot Chocolate, 38
  in Creepy-Crawly Cake, 10
  in Madagascar Hissing Cockroach Cakes, 20
Chocolate chips
  in Blood and Bile Cocktail, 36
Chow mein noodles
  in Scorpions, 28
  in Scrumptious Squid Slush, 48
  in Tasty Tarantula Feast, 14
Cicadas, 29
Cocoa powder
  in Cow's Blood Hot Chocolate, 38
  in Creepy-Crawly Cake, 10
Coconut
  in Tasty Tarantula Feast, 14
Cow's Blood Hot Chocolate, 38
Cow Tongue Chow, 34
Cream
  in Creepy-Crawly Cake, 10
  in Great Big Blob, The, 58
Cream cheese
  in Cow Tongue Chow, 34
  with Putrid Pizza, 54
  with Tomato Hornworm Juice, 17
  in Scrumptious Squid Slush, 48
  in Slimy Centipede Salad, 18
  on Slippery Octopus Salad, 50

Creepy-Crawly Cake, 10
Crushed Grasshopper Guacamole, 12
Cucumbers
  in Slimy Centipede Salad, 18
Currants
  on Bloody Rat Legs, 42

E
Eggs
  100-Year-Old Eggs, 46
  in Cow Tongue Chow, 34
  in Giant Sea Slug Sandwich, 56
  in Pig's Brain Pancakes, 32
Eyeball Kabobs, 39

F
Fettuccine
  in Slippery Octopus Salad, 50
Firm Worm Dessert, 22
Frosting
  on Creepy-Crawly Cake, 10
  on Madagascar Hissing Cockroach Cakes, 20
Fruit leather
  on Cicadas, 29

G
Garlic salt
  in Crushed Grasshopper Guacamole, 12
Gelatin
  with Blood and Bile Cocktail, 38
  Firm Worm Dessert, 22
  Great Big Blob, The, 58
  in Sea Slug Smoothie, 52
Giant Sea Slug Sandwich, 56
Grapes
  in Blood and Bile Cocktail, 36
Great Big Blob, The, 58
Ground beef
  in Rat Stew, 40
Guacamole
  Crushed Grasshopper Guacamole, 12
Gummy worms
  with Cow's Blood Hot Chocolate, 38
  in Creepy-Crawly Cake, 10
  in Firm Worm Dessert, 22

H
Ham
  in Pig's Brain Pancakes, 32
Honey
  in Ant Attack Ade, 16
  in Giant Sea Slug Sandwich, 56
  with Sand Crab Snacks, 53
Hot chocolate
  Cow's Blood Hot Chocolate, 38

J
Jam
  on Cow Tongue Chow, 34
Jicama
  in Crushed Grasshopper Guacamole, 12
Juice
  Ant Attack Ade, 16
  Blood and Bile Cocktail, 36
  Sea Slug Smoothie, 52
  Tomato Hornworm Juice, 17

K
Kabobs
  Eyeball Kabobs, 39

L
Lettuce
  in Crushed Grasshopper Guacamole, 12
  in Slimy Centipede Salad, 18
  in Scrumptious Squid Slush, 48
Licorice
  in Ant Attack Ade, 16
  in Great Big Blob, The, 58

M
Madagascar Hissing Cockroach Cakes, 20
Malted milk balls
  in Madagascar Hissing Cockroach Cakes, 20
Maple syrup
  with Pig's Brain Pancakes, 32
Marshmallows
  in Cow's Blood Hot Chocolate, 38
  see Scorpions, 28
Milk
  in Cow's Blood Hot Chocolate, 38
  in Pig's Brain Pancakes, 32
  with Putrid Pizza, 54
  in Sea Slug Smoothie, 52
Mushrooms
  on Putrid Pizza, 54
Mustard
  with Giant Sea Slug Sandwich, 56

N
Noodles
  in Scorpions, 28
  in Scrumptious Squid Slush, 48
  in Slippery Octopus Salad, 50
  in Squirmy Wormy Spaghetti, 24
  in Tasty Tarantula Feast, 14

O
Olives
  in Crushed Grasshopper Guacamole, 12
  in Eyeball Kabobs, 39
  in Giant Sea Slug Sandwich, 56
  in Rat Stew, 40
  in Sand Crab Snacks, 53
  in Scrumptious Squid Slush, 48
  in Slippery Octopus Salad, 50
  in Squirmy Wormy Spaghetti, 24
Onion
  in Crushed Grasshopper Guacamole, 12
Onion rings
  in Rat Stew, 40
Orange juice
  in Ant Attack Ade, 16

P
Pad thai
  see Tasty Tarantula Feast, 14
Pancakes
  Pig's Brain Pancakes, 32
Peanuts
  in Tasty Tarantula Feast, 14
Peanut butter
  Slugs, 26
  Worms, 27
Pesto
  with Eyeball Kabobs, 39
Pig's Brain Pancakes, 32
Pistachio nuts
  in Eyeball Kabobs, 39
Pizza
  Putrid Pizza, 54
Potato chips
  Sand Crab Snacks, 53
Pretzel sticks
  in Madagascar Hissing Cockroach Cakes, 20
  in Slimy Centipede Salad, 18
Putrid Pizza, 54

R
Raisins
  on Bloody Rat Legs, 42
Radishes
  in Rat Stew, 40
Raspberry sauce
  on Great Big Blob, The, 58
  with Pig's Brain Pancakes, 32
Rat Stew, 40
Red peppers
  on Giant Sea Slug Sandwich, 56

S
Salads
  Scrumptious Squid Slush, 48
  Slimy Centipede Salad, 18
  Slippery Octopus Salad, 50
Sand Crab Snacks, 53
Sandwich
  Giant Sea Slug Sandwich, 56
Sauerkraut
  in Rat Stew, 40
Sausage
  in Giant Sea Slug Sandwich, 56
  in Tasty Tarantula Feast, 14
Scorpions, 28
Scrumptious Squid Slush, 48
Sea Slug Smoothie, 52
Shrimp
  in Scrumptious Squid Slush, 48
Slimy Centipede Salad, 18
Slippery Octopus Salad, 50
Slugs, 26
Smoothies
  Ant Attack Ade, 16
  Sea Slug Smoothie, 52
Spaghetti
  Squirmy Wormy Spaghetti, 24
Spinach
  in 100-Year-Old Eggs, 46
  in Slippery Octopus Salad, 50
Sponge cakes
  see Madagascar Hissing Cockroach C...
Squirmy Wormy Spaghetti, 24
Stew
  Rat Stew, 40
Strawberries
  in Ant Attack Ade, 16
Syrup, maple
  with Pig's Brain Pancakes, 32

T
Tasty Tarantula Feast, 14
Tomatoes
  in Eyeball Kabobs, 39
  on Putrid Pizza, 54
  in Rat Stew, 40
  in Scrumptious Squid Slush, 48
  in Slippery Octopus Salad, 50
Tomato juice
  Tomato Hornworm Juice, 17
Tomato sauce
  with Eyeball Kabobs, 39
  in Rat Stew, 40
  in Squirmy Wormy Spaghetti, 24
Tortilla chips
  with Crushed Grasshopper Guacamo...
Turkey
  in Tasty Tarantula Feast, 14

U
Udon noodles
  in Squirmy Wormy Spaghetti, 24

W
Worms, 27

Y
Yogurt
  in Ant Attack Ade, 16
  in Sea Slug Smoothie, 52